Deep Sea Doctor Dean

Author and Illustrator: Leo Timmers

Clavis

NEW YORK

Like he did every morning, Doctor Dean
dove into the ocean in his special submarine
looking for fish and other sea animals in trouble.
From a mackerel with a sore tail,
to a sardine with a foul smell,
to a jellyfish with a backache,
Doctor Dean knows the cure.
Soon his first patient will swim along …

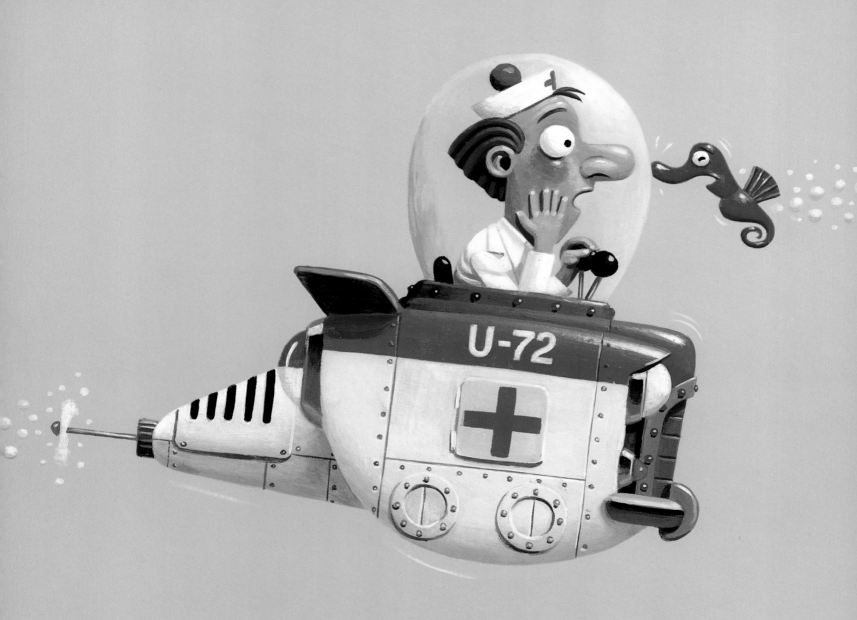

"Whoa, Sea Horse, be careful!" Doctor Dean shouted
while stepping on his brakes.
"I am Sea *Race*horse!"
the little, red, sea horse whinnied proudly.
"I am the fastest fish in the ocean!
Only, I can't see very well, Doctor.
Almost nothing, to be honest."

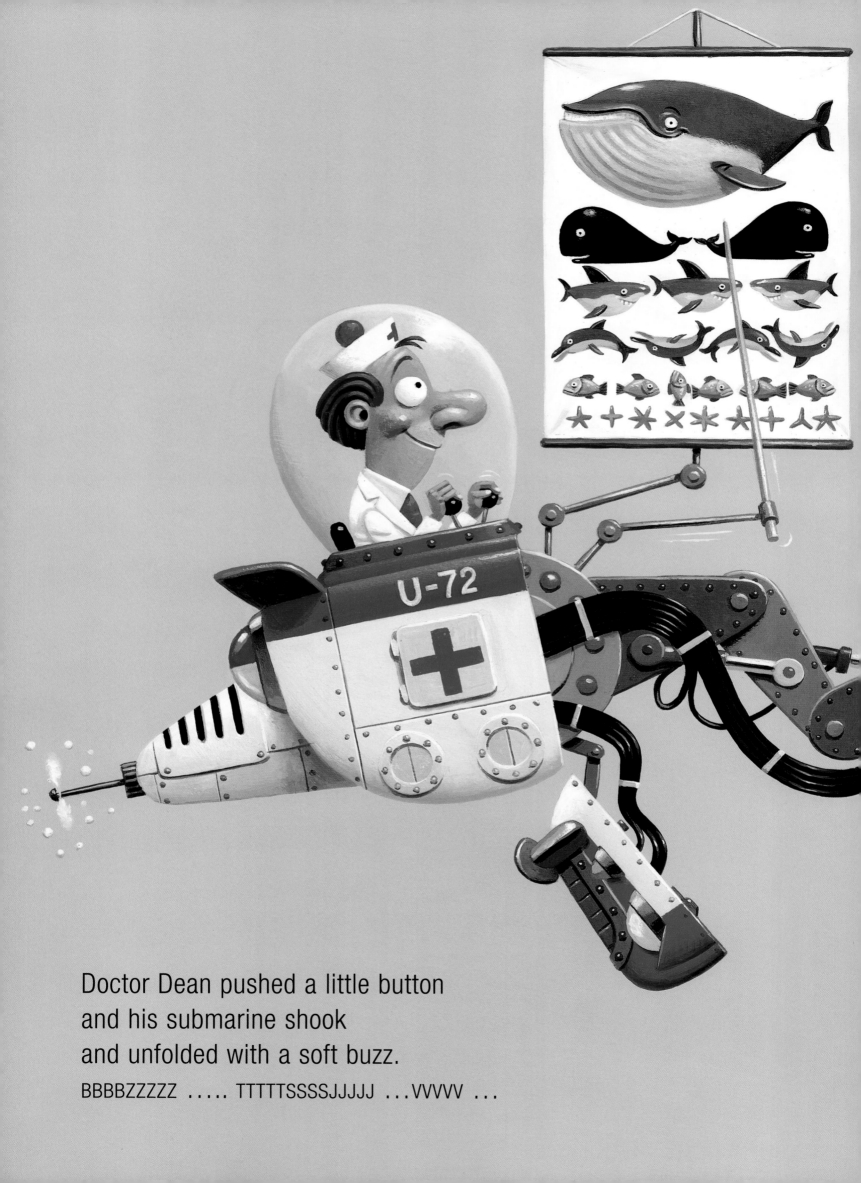

Doctor Dean pushed a little button
and his submarine shook
and unfolded with a soft buzz.
BBBBZZZZZ ..... TTTTTSSSSJJJJJ ...VVVVV ...

Doctor Dean immediately saw what was wrong and said,
"You need glasses, lad."
Sea Racehorse picked out a pair that wouldn't fall from his nose.
He couldn't believe how much better his eyesight was now.
"Thanks a lot, doctor," he yelled.
"My pleasure," Doctor Dean said, smiling.
And off Doctor Dean dove, deeper into the ocean.

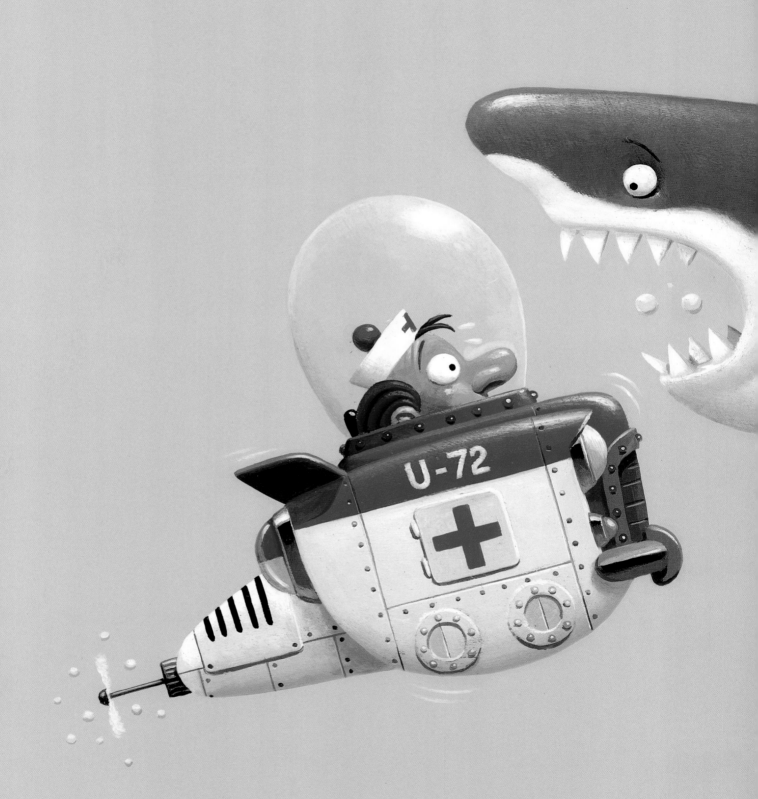

Suddenly, a mouth full of razor-sharp teeth
popped-up in front of Doctor Dean.
"Don't be hafraid, Hoctor, hi have such a
hoothache!" Shark jabbered.
"A toothache?" Doctor Dean gulped,
getting over his fright.
"Hes, hoothache. Hi cannot hite anymore."

BBBBBBZZZZZ .... TTTTSSSSJJJJJJJJJJ ... VVVVVV ....
"Please, sit down," Doctor Dean said, "and open your mouth."
He found the rotten tooth easily and pulled it out.
Relieved, Shark chattered his enormous teeth.
"Brush them well," Doctor Dean recommended.
"Thanks a lot!" Shark said with a broad smile.
"My pleasure, pal!"

All of a sudden, it got very dark.

"And who have we got here?" Doctor Dean asked in friendly manner.

"It's me, Doctor," Octopus moaned. "My legs hurt terribly.
I was playing tag with a school of sticklebacks."

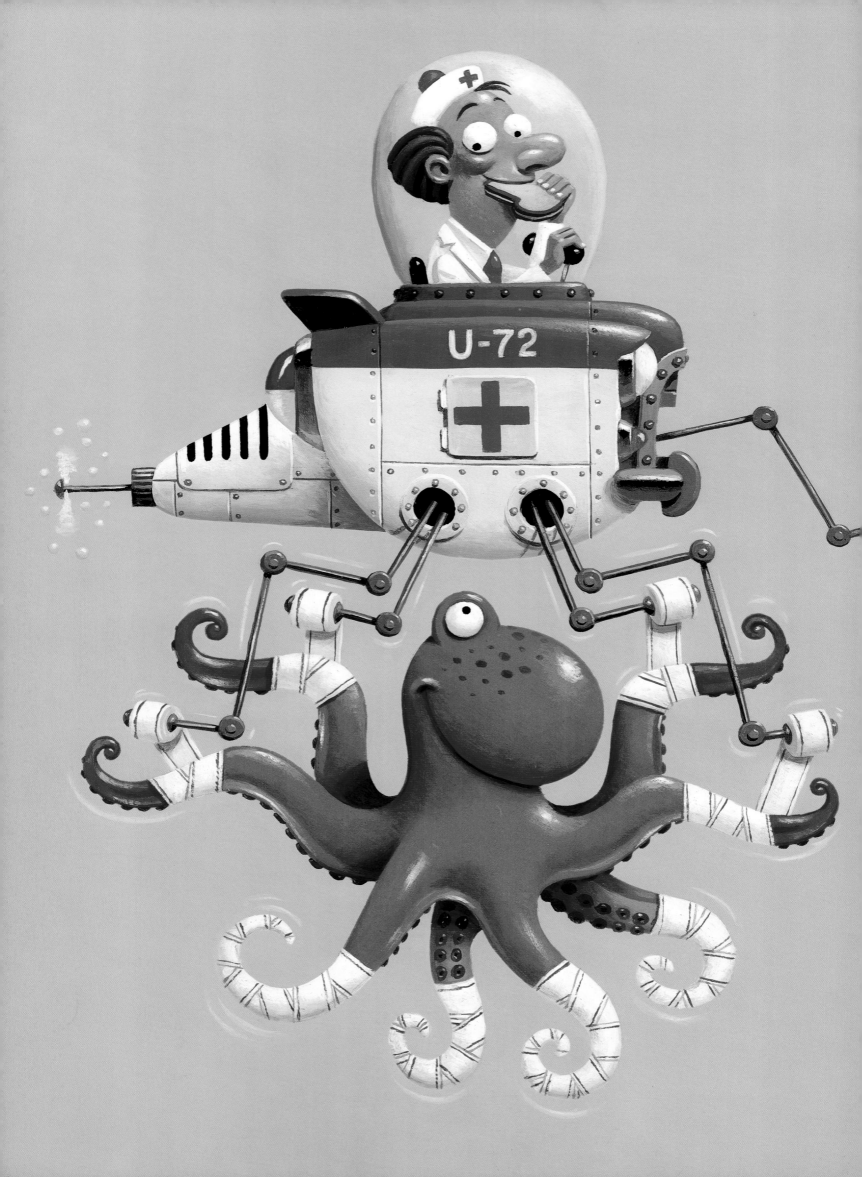

BBBBBBZZZZZ .... TTTTSSSSJJJJJJJJJJ ... VVVVVV...
Doctor Dean rubbed some ointment on Octopus's legs
and applied eight bandages.
"In a couple of days you'll be your old self again, Octo."
Octopus cheerfully wiggled all his arms.
"It already hurts less, Doctor. Thanks!"
"My pleasure," Doctor Dean said.

Doctor Dean was almost at bottom of the ocean.
In between seaweed he saw Whale.
"Hello Whale. Why are you so sad?" he asked gently.
Whale didn't answer.
"Could I be of assistance?" Doctor Dean tried again.
"Oh," Whale sighed, "just leave me alone."

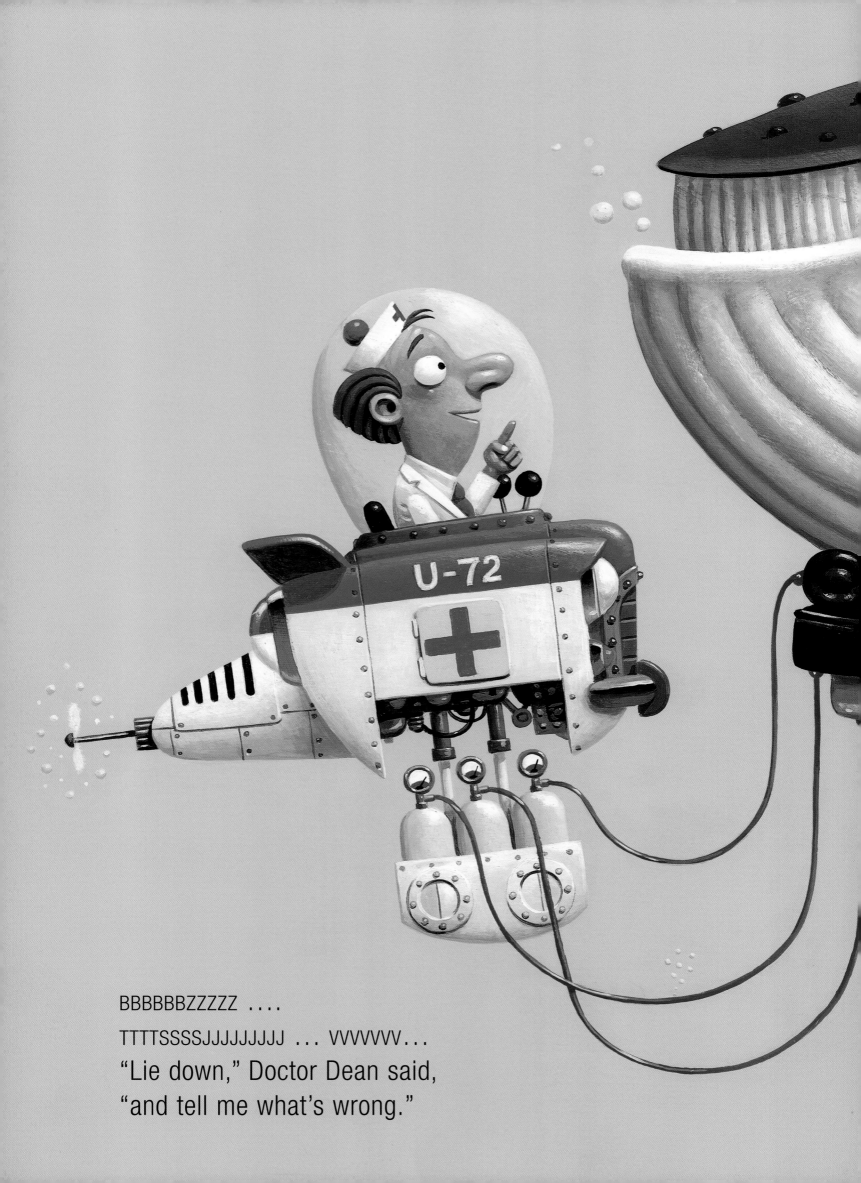

BBBBBBZZZZZ . . . .

TTTTSSSSJJJJJJJJJ . . . VVVVVV. . .

"Lie down," Doctor Dean said,
"and tell me what's wrong."

"All the fish are so slender and agile," Whale wailed.
"But not me. I'm fat and slow. Not a real fish at all."
"But, Whale, you're the biggest and strongest of all.
Everyone thinks you're a magnificent!"
"Do you think so, Doctor? Really?"
Whale's eyes sparkled. Feeling good again, he swam off.
Doctor Dean watched him and whispered, "My pleasure."

It had been a busy day.
Doctor Dean pulled the lever of his submarine
to break the surface, but the submarine didn't move.
He revved the engine at full blast,
but it didn't move.
"I'm stuck!" Doctor Dean called. "Help!"

With his new glasses Sea Racehorse had seen
everything happen from far.
"Don't worry, I'll get help," he assured Doctor Dean,
and off he went like a thoroughbred.

Soon, Sea Racehorse returned with Shark.
"Shall I give you a hand, Doctor?" Shark asked.
And with one big bite, his healthy teeth cut the submarine loose.
"Oh no!" Sea Racehorse shouted. "The engine!"

There was a loud bang and Doctor Dean's
submarine began to sink quickly.
He crashed on the bottom of the ocean.
"I'll be right back," Sea Racehorse shouted
as he galloped away.

This time Sea Racehorse came back with Octopus,
who began repairing the engine in double-quick time.
His eight arms didn't hurt anymore.
"Start the engine!" Octopus ordered, but nothing happened.
"I don't feel so well," Doctor Dean muttered.
The bang had rattled him terribly.
"He has to go up," Shark said, "but how?"

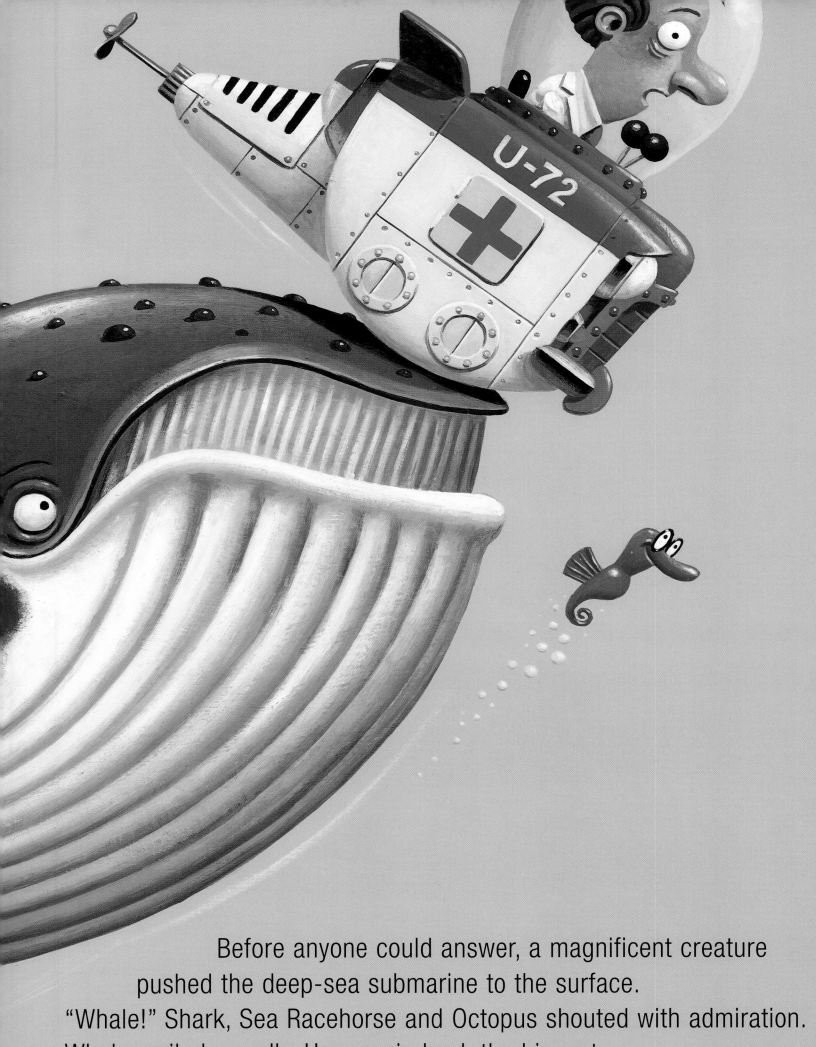

Before anyone could answer, a magnificent creature
pushed the deep-sea submarine to the surface.
"Whale!" Shark, Sea Racehorse and Octopus shouted with admiration.
Whale smiled proudly. He was, indeed, the biggest
and strongest of the ocean, just as Doctor Dean had said.

When he broke through the surface,
Doctor Dean had to take a second to recover.
He looked at his rescuers one by one and said,
"Thank you, Sea Racehorse, Shark, Octopus and Whale!
Without you, it wouldn't have ended well."
The four rescuers smiled and shouted: "Our pleasure, Doctor Dean!"

To my parents

Deep Sea Doctor Dean by Leo Timmers
translated from Dutch.
Original title: Diepzee dokter Diederik

ISBN: 978 1 60537 006 4

Manufactured in China
First Edition
10 9 8 7 6 5 4 3 2 1